MW01046013

# SHORT TALES CLASSICS

## L. Frank Baum's

# The Wonderful Wizard of Oz

## The Cyclone

## Adapted by Rob M. Worley
## Illustrated by Mike Dubisch

**GREEN LEVEL**

- Familiar topics
- Frequently used words
- Repeating language patterns

**BLUE LEVEL**

- New ideas introduced
- Larger vocabulary
- Variety of language patterns

**PINK LEVEL**

- More complex ideas
- Extended vocabulary
- Expanded sentence structures

To learn more about Short Tales leveling, go to www.abdopublishing.com

Published by Magic Wagon, a division of the ABDO Publishing Group, 8000 West 78th Street, Edina, Minnesota, 55439. Copyright © 2008 by Abdo Consulting Group, Inc. International copyrights reserved in all countries. All rights reserved. No part of this book may be reproduced in any form without written permission from the publisher. Short Tales ™ is a trademark and logo of Magic Wagon.

Printed in the United States.

Written by L. Frank Baum
Adapted Text by Rob M. Worley
Illustrations by Mike Dubisch
Colors by Wes Hartman
Edited by Stephanie Hedlund
Interior Layout by Kristen Fitzner Denton
Book Design and Packaging by Shannon Eric Denton

**Library of Congress Cataloging-in-Publication Data**
Worley, Rob M.
  L. Frank Baum's the wonderful wizard of Oz : the cyclone / adapted by Rob M. Worley ; illustrated by Michael Dubisch.
     p. cm. -- (Short tales classics)
  ISBN 978-1-60270-124-3
  [1. Tornadoes--Fiction. 2. Fantasy.] I. Dubisch, Michael, ill. II. Baum, L. Frank (Lyman Frank), 1856-1919. Wizard of Oz. III. Title. IV. Title: Wonderful wizard of Oz. V. Title: Cyclone.
PZ7.W887625Lf 2008
[E]--dc22
                              2007036985

# Contents

# CHAPTER ONE: DOROTHY'S NEW HOME

Dorothy was an orphan. So, she was sent to Kansas to live with her Uncle Henry and her Auntie Em.

They lived in a farmhouse that Uncle Henry had built.

"Can I help you?" Dorothy asked.

"There's nothing you can do," replied Uncle Henry. "You're just a little girl."

Then, Uncle Henry put a trapdoor in the floor.

He dug a large hole under the trapdoor. He placed a ladder for them to climb down.

"This cellar will protect us from cyclones," said Uncle Henry.

When Dorothy looked out her front door, she saw only the flat prairie.

Not a tree nor a house disrupted the flat country.

The stretch of dull, gray land seemed to go on forever.

Only Dorothy's dog, Toto, could make her laugh.

Toto was never dull. They played all day long and Dorothy loved him dearly.

"We might as well play," Dorothy told Toto.

Toto touched his cold little nose against her cheek and then licked it.

## CHAPTER TWO: THE CYCLONE

One day, Dorothy and Toto did not have time to play.

They heard a low wail of the wind. The long prairie grass bowed in waves before the coming storm.

"There's a cyclone coming, Em!" shouted Uncle Henry.

"Quick, Dorothy!" yelled Auntie Em. "Run for the cellar!"

Auntie Em was terrified. She hurriedly threw open the cellar trapdoor.

Dorothy hugged Toto tight.

She tried to follow her aunt down the ladder.

Toto was terrified, too.

He jumped from Dorothy's arms and ran away.

Dorothy chased after him.

"Hurry, Dorothy!" called Auntie Em.

Dorothy found Toto hiding under the bed.

"I can't let the cyclone take Toto!" she cried out.

She grabbed Toto, but it was too late!

A great wind shook the house.

The house shook so hard that Dorothy lost her balance.
She fell suddenly upon the floor.

Then a strange thing happened.

# CHAPTER THREE:
# THE FLYING HOUSE

The house whirled around
and around.

It rose slowly through the air.

Dorothy felt as if she were
going up in a balloon.

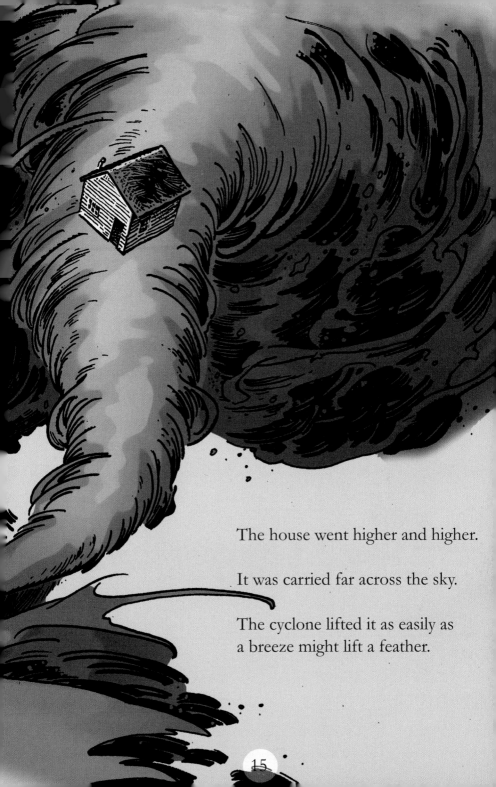

The house went higher and higher.

It was carried far across the sky.

The cyclone lifted it as easily as
a breeze might lift a feather.

Inside it got very dark and the wind howled.

To Dorothy, the ride was quite gentle.

But Toto did not like it one bit!

He ran about the room, barking at the wind.

Toto got too close to the trapdoor.

"Look out, Toto!" Dorothy cried.

The little dog slipped through the opening.

Dorothy was terrified that her friend had fallen to the ground!

# CHAPTER FOUR: TOTO IS SAVED

The strong winds held Toto up.

He flew around and around in the middle of the cyclone.

It would have been fun if Toto weren't so terrified.

Dorothy was sure Toto would fall eventually.

When he passed close by, she grabbed his ear.

She carefully pulled him back into the house.

Dorothy slammed the trapdoor shut.

"You scared me, Toto!" she scolded the dog.

But, they were both relieved that he was back inside.

Dorothy lay down on her bed.

Toto snuggled beside her.

"What will happen to us, Toto?" the girl asked her friend.

Hour after hour passed by.  Dorothy got over her fright.

The house rocked and swayed in the center of the cyclone.

Soon, Dorothy and Toto fell fast asleep.

Dorothy was awakened by a sudden shock.

She and Toto bounced up into the air.

They landed on the soft bed.

# CHAPTER FIVE: A SUDDEN LANDING

Dorothy sat up.

"I wonder what happened," she said.

She noticed that the house was not moving.

And it was no longer dark. Bright sunshine flooded the little room.

Dorothy threw open the door.

She expected to see the dull, gray plains of Kansas.

Instead, Dorothy saw the most beautiful land.

All around was green grass.

Tall trees bore bright red fruit, and flowers displayed
a rainbow of colors.

Birds with beautifully painted feathers flew about.

"Where are we, Toto?" Dorothy asked, eyes wide with wonder.

She had never seen birds of such color flying over the gray prairies of Kansas.

## CHAPTER SIX: THE MUNCHKINS

Dorothy saw a number of strange little people by a brook.

They were looking at Dorothy with hopeful expressions.

The little people all bowed toward Dorothy.

The men stood back and a woman approached.

"Welcome, most noble witch, to the land of the Oz," she said.

"We are the Munchkins and we thank you heartily!" said one of the men.

"You have killed the Wicked Witch of the East!" said another.

"You have set us free!" said the old woman.

The Munchkins lifted Dorothy to celebrate their new hero.

"Oh, dear!" said Dorothy.

Dorothy was sure she had neither killed a witch nor freed any Munchkins.

She was, after all, just a little girl.